Opening Night

by Rachel Kranz

illustrated by Anita DuFalla

TABLE OF CONTENTS

CHAPTER 1

Will I Get the Part?

Dear Diary,

I'm so excited! I just heard that Ms. Chen, our drama teacher, is going to put on a play called *The Princess in the Kitchen.* We'll rehearse after school, then put on our show for three nights in a row. All the kids and parents and families will come!

When I told my friend Lupe how excited I was, she shook her head so that her long, curly black hair flew back and forth.

"Don't get too excited, Julia," she said. "You don't even know yet if you'll get the part."

Lupe thinks she's so smart. I told her she'd better start being nicer to me. Because I'm going to be the princess—that's the best part. And then everyone will want to be my friend! Besides, I want to be an actress when I grow up, so being a star will be a good experience for me.

Dear Diary,

Lupe didn't want to have lunch with me today. She said she's tired of hearing about the play.

"Like I care!" I said. I looked down at Lupe—I am taller than she is. "Fine!" I told her. "I have to learn my poem anyway!" (We all have to say poems for the tryouts.)

Dear Diary,

It's a lot of work learning this poem! I didn't think it would be so hard.

I don't care. Once I get the part, it will all be worth it. I'll wear a beautiful princess dress, and everybody will say how gorgeous I look. And Lupe will be sorry she was so mean to me, but then it will be too late.

Dear Diary,

The tryouts were today! I had to stand up in front of a whole roomful of people and say my poem. The play isn't just for third graders. Fourth graders and fifth graders will be in it, too. So there were lots of big kids listening to me and at first I was really scared. But somehow I got through it.

Ms. Chen smiled at me when I was finished. I just know she'll give me the part! I can't wait until tomorrow!

When I got done with tryouts, I looked around for Lupe. Sometimes she has soccer practice after school, and I wait for her. So I thought maybe she would wait for me after tryouts.

But she wasn't there. Oh, well. She'll be the one who's sorry when she sees how beautiful I look on the stage!

Dear Diary,

I GOT THE PART!!! I GOT THE PART!!! I GOT THE PART!!!

This is how I feel inside: **!!++$$!!** In other words, I feel GREAT!

Ms. Chen had posted the list of characters on the bulletin board outside her classroom. There was a big group of kids all crowding around, and for a minute I was too scared even to look. But then I pushed my way up to the bulletin board.

And there was my name, right at the top of the list! I was so excited, I felt like I couldn't even breathe!

Then something weird happened. I saw Lupe at the other end of the hall, watching. She looked worried. I wasn't sure if she was hoping I would get the part or that I wouldn't! But when I smiled and waved my hands over my head to show that I got it, she gave me a big grin and waved her hands, too.

Then, by the time I got over to where she was, she had gone. If she was so happy I got the part, why didn't she wait for me?

CHAPTER 2

This Isn't What I Expected!

Dear Diary,

I expected that being in the play would be fun, but it's awful!

First, there are all these lines to learn. I thought it would be fun to have the biggest part in the play. I didn't know I would have more work than anybody else!

Second, remember that beautiful princess dress I was going to wear? Well, guess what? This princess is in disguise for the whole entire play! She doesn't get to wear pretty clothes! That's the point. She is stuck in the kitchen wearing greasy, dirty rags—and that is the costume I have to wear! It's not fair!!!

Dear Diary,

I tried to talk to Ms. Chen about the play. I thought maybe I could get her to cut some of my lines so I wouldn't have so much work to do. But she just laughed and said, "That's usually the way it is with big parts—they are a lot of work!"

Then I asked if I could wear a different costume. Maybe the princess has a special pretty dress that she wears some of the time.

But Ms. Chen just shook her head and said, "That's not the way it works. You have to wear the costume that fits the part."

So then I said, "Well, maybe I won't be in your old play, then! Maybe I'll just quit right now!"

Ms. Chen looked very serious.

"Is that really what you want to do, Julia?" she said quietly. "You want to quit?"

"Maybe!" I said. I tried to look as if I didn't care. "Maybe that is exactly what I want to do!"

"All right," said Ms. Chen. "I'll give you one day to think it over. You can tell me your decision tomorrow."

So I went home. And there was Mama on the phone, talking long-distance to Tía Miriam and Tío Jorge, my aunt and uncle.

"Ay, bendito, Miriam!" Mama was saying. "Not just a part—the best part! Yes, Jorge, that's right! Our Julita is a star!"

Mama put her hand over the receiver. "They're going to make a special trip just to see you, Julita," she told me. "We're all so proud!"

Well, that settled it. I couldn't quit now. I went up to my room to work on my part. I hate memorizing all these lines. I just hate it!

Dear Diary,

I almost called Lupe today. I thought, maybe she really didn't like how much I was bragging about the play before. But I sure don't feel like bragging now! Maybe if I tell her how everything has gone wrong, she'll be my friend again.

But I didn't call her. I was too embarrassed.

Dear Diary,

Today at rehearsal, I couldn't remember any of my lines. I had to ask Ms. Chen for help every single time!

Finally, I heard Johnny Simon whisper to Jason Bunche, "She better learn her lines by opening night, or this play is gonna be three hours long!" I just wanted to sink through the floor and disappear!

Dear Diary,

Well, I did it. I finally learned my lines. It took hours and hours of hard, hard, really hard work, but now I feel like I could say them in my sleep!

You know, I figured out something interesting. At the beginning of the play, the princess is very proud and snobbish. She acts like she's better than everyone else.

Then she has to work in the kitchen, in disguise, so she can find out why the mean prime minister wants to steal the throne.

But something happens to her when she works so hard. She learns to be nicer to people. She makes friends with the other kitchen maid. I like her a lot more at the end of the play than at the beginning!

So maybe it's good for people to work hard. After all, at the end of the play, the princess doesn't just save the kingdom. She makes a new friend, and she didn't have any friends before because she thought she was better than everyone else.

Dear Diary,

I think about this princess character all the time. I want to show the audience that she is different at the end of the play than at the beginning. Just getting the lines right won't be enough. I have to really make them know how she's feeling.

CHAPTER 3

Here Comes Opening Night!

Dear Diary,

Opening night is in two days! At least I know my lines now. In fact, the other day, Johnny forgot his line. After a minute, I whispered it to him very softly so no one else would know.

He looked totally surprised. "Thanks, Julia!" he said to me after rehearsal. "Giving me my line that way, that was cool."

Now I was surprised. "Sure," I said. "No problem." What did he think I was going to do—embarrass him in front of the whole cast?

Dear Diary,

Opening night is tomorrow! I am SO SCARED!

I told Johnny that I was really nervous and he said, "Don't worry, Julia. You won't make any mistakes. Look how well you know your lines!"

"I'm not worried about making any mistakes or forgetting my lines," I told him. "I'm worried that I won't show people what this princess is really like. I want them to see that she has really changed."

What I said to Johnny made me think about me and Lupe. Now I think the reason she didn't wait for me the day I found out I got the part was that I was acting stuck-up and treating her like she wasn't important. I guess I've changed, too, and I want her to know it. But I'm afraid she won't want to talk to me if I call her.

Dear Diary,

Opening night is tonight. I just came home from school, and there were Tía Miriam and Tío Jorge in the living room.

"We're so excited, Julia!" Tía Miriam said.

"Yes," said Tío Jorge. "Our big star!"

"I'm not really the star," I said. "Lots of people worked on this show."

"Yes," said Tía Miriam, "but you are the most important, yes?"

"No," I said. "In this show, everybody is important."

Mama gave me a big smile. "All right, Julita," she said. "Why don't you go up and rest before dinner? You have a big night tonight."

So I came up here, but I'm really not ready to rest yet. There's just one more thing I have to do.

Dear Diary,

Well, I did it. I finally called Lupe.

Only she wasn't home. Nobody was. The answering machine was on.

So I left her a message. I said I was sorry if I acted like she wasn't important. I said I missed her. I said that I hoped she'd come to the play tonight, and I hoped she still wanted to be my friend.

Dear Diary,

Opening night is over. This has been the most amazing night of my life!

When I got to the school auditorium, I was really nervous. What would Tío Jorge and Tía Miriam think of the play? Would

Papa and Mama like it?? What if somebody made a mistake??? What if I made a mistake????

Then it was time. I took a deep breath and walked onstage. The lights were very bright and hot. I could feel the audience out there, listening. I knew that my family was in the front row. I wondered if Lupe was there.

But I knew I couldn't think about any of that. I just had to think about the princess. I had to show what she was really like.

I said my first line. Then I just kept saying my lines. Then it was over. Everybody was clapping and cheering. I could hear my whole family shout, "JULIA!"

Then we walked backstage.

I wondered if I had done a good job. The audience was applauding, but did they understand about the princess?

Then, all of a sudden, Lupe was there! "Oh, Julia," she said, "that was great! You made the princess seem so real. It was like watching a real person! I felt like I knew her!"

"You did know her," I said. "She was just like me—mean. But then she learned how to be nice. I learned my lesson, too, Lupe. I'll never be mean to you again."

"Then we're still friends?" Lupe said.

"Forever," I told her.

I'm not sure I still want to be an actress when I grow up, but I'm sure glad I was in this play.